Rocina Leitão

Gary R. Lowell

Full Moon Publishing, LLC

Glade Spring, VA

Website http://www.fullmoonpublishingllc

Edited by Jamie White and CP Bialois

Cover Photo by Gary R. Lowell

ISBN: 0692580182
ISBN-13: 978-0692580189

Colin St. Andrew MacLorey was drunk, not eloquently or pugnaciously drunk as sometimes happens, but indisputably drunk all the same. This was an almost nightly occurrence at Casa dos Doces, a bar and brothel located at the intersection of Rua Aurelio Pinto and Rua Matadouro in Fundão, Portugal. Fundão itself is a small but attractive city of white houses and red-tiled roofs nestled in the mountains of east-central Portugal. It is also the gateway to the Panasqueira mine located some twenty-five kilometers west of the city. This mine has been the major producer of tungsten and tin ores in all of Europe since the 1890's and is still in production to this day.

The location of Casa dos Doces was not ideal for a brothel which ought to be discreetly situated five or six kilometers out of town. Indeed, for the fifty years prior to 1940, this building served as the sole *mercado de ferragens,* or hardware store, for Fundão. However, all tungsten concentrates from the Panasqueira mine passed along Rua Aurelio Pinto through Fundão by truck convoys to reach the outside world via Guarda, a much larger city located about sixty kilometers north of Fundão on a major east-west highway.

After the fall of France on June 22nd of 1940, ore concentrates destined for Germany were transported east from Guarda by truck to Vilar Formoso, the major Portuguese border crossing into Spain. Here, the concentrates were loaded onto high priority German trains, the so-called "Nazi ghost trains", and taken across Franco's Spain via Salamanca to Vichy France and finally into Germany. Identical amounts of ore concentrates were delivered to Britain by truck convoys turning west at Guarda and proceeding two hundred-twenty kilometers through Viseu to Porto where British ships waited. So, in fact, the Casa dos Doces was ideally located because its principal mission was not to provide booze and sex to lonely miners, but to monitor all tungsten shipments leaving the Panasqueira mine on behalf of the gentle leaders of the Third Reich.

Tungsten, or wolfram as it is generally known in Europe, is element number seventy-four on the periodic table and symbolized by W. It is a remarkable metal for imparting high strength, hardness, and heat resistance to steel because it has the highest melting point of any pure metal at three thousand four hundred and twenty-two degrees Celsius. These properties made it an object of necessity for the war machines of both Allies and Axis powers for tank armor, tool steel, ignition points, gun barrels, and the like. Consequently, both sides felt compelled to compete for neutral Portugal's precious tungsten exports, each attempting to discredit the other while trying to curry favor with the fascist dictator, António de Oliveira Salazar, in hopes of obtaining more than their rightful share.

These competing and opposed efforts required spies, many spies evidently, as well as paid informants and Portuguese secret police agents to keep track of the surreptitious activities of all of these spies. In fact, there were so many foreign spies that local cynics said Portugal ought to be in the business of exporting them instead of wolfram. Not all foreigners in Portugal were spies, of course. Some were escaping British, Canadian, and, later in the war, American prisoners of war. Others were displaced royals, but most were Jewish refugees seeking sanctuary from well-known Nazi atrocities. Still, it meant a lot of British and German spies were digging in the garden, especially in Lisbon and

Fundão.

The Germans felt they had to ensure that they received their full measure of tungsten guaranteed by treaty with Portugal while the Brits naturally felt they had to be equally certain that the Germans did not get a kilogram more than this amount. Of course, Germany could have invaded Portugal without much opposition from the British and seized the mine, but the big thinkers in Berlin feared this would disrupt and perhaps even shut down mine production entirely. The Reich wisely chose to honor Portugal's neutrality.

It followed that economic competition between Allies and Axis powers triggered rapid increases in wolfram price and, consequently, also production at the mine as well as certain illegal black market activities by so-called Portuguese *"wolframistas"*. As a result, the number of mine workers, the population of Fundão, and the brothel business at Casa dos Doces grew in direct proportion to the snowballing market price of tungsten metal.

Of course, the Portuguese miners and millworkers at the Panasqueira mine did not care who got what as far as that went. They were paid to extract large, lustrous, black crystals of wolframite from more than one thousand relatively thin, flat-lying quartz veins injected near the contacts of a two hundred-ninety million-year-old granite body that intruded into older schist. These veins also carried cassiterite, the most important ore of tin which, although subordinate to wolframite in production tonnage, was also a strategic metal and war-time necessity for all of the belligerent parties. The gangue, or non-economic waste material, includes more than fifty mineral species, among them tourmaline, fluorite, muscovite, arsenopyrite, quartz, and topaz. Today, one often sees spectacular specimens of large, well-formed crystals of these gangue minerals from Panasqueira proudly displayed in private collections, commercial rock shops, and museums all over the world.

After impurities are removed from the wolframite ore at the mine site, the resulting powdered wolframite concentrate carries about 75 weight percent WO_3. This compound, WO_3, is tungsten trioxide and it is the marketing form for tungsten from all tungsten mines in the world. WO_3 is itself 79.3 weight percent tungsten, but the pure tungsten metal is actually recovered at off-site refineries chosen by industrial customers.

MacLorey was a large man at a height of six feet four inches tall and two hundred-thirty pounds, or sixteen-point-four stone if you prefer British measure, and he had a correspondingly large capacity for food, women, and alcohol. This made him a popular and valued patron at Casa dos Doces. Of course, his size, pale freckled skin, blue eyes, square shaven jaw, and orange military-style haircut made him stand out as a foreigner; a rather handsome foreigner according to the ladies of Casa dos Doces. This is not to say that his imperfect Portuguese spoken through a pronounced Scottish accent did not also reveal him as a foreigner. A Brit in this part of the world at this time in history, almost always equated with spy and indeed this was the case.

Captain MacLorey was a thirty-two–year-old Gaelic-speaking native of the Isle of Skye with a doctorate in economic geology from Edinburgh University. His dissertation subject dealt with tin and tungsten deposits of the Saint Austell Granite in Cornwall, England and it was precisely for this reason that the Economic Warfare Section of MI-6 sent the Captain to monitor Nazi tungsten activities in Fundão.

MacLorey made frequent trips to the Panasqueira mine and bi-weekly visits to Lisbon to report to his MI-6 bosses, and when he returned he always checked in at the Doces to drink and visit the ladies. His duties brought him into nearly daily contact with Senhor Gerhardt Framlow, the proprietor of Casa dos Doces.

Herr Doktor Gerhardt Framlow sat in a comfortable chair at a round table beneath a slowly revolving ceiling fan in a corner of the bar room of Casa dos Doces. He was engaged in examination of an account book and narrowly observing Captain MacLorey. Framlow was MacLorey's opposite in nearly all respects. He was a brilliant metallurgist and an articulate man in several languages, but he was also small, crooked, and rather ugly.

Medically and physiologically speaking, Framlow could not in any way be considered a dwarf, but this fact did not prevent the local wits from calling him *o duende feio*, the ugly dwarf. His dangling waxed mustachios made it appear as if he harbored two good-sized mice in his mouth and he wore a monocle that he did not need for effect. This steely accessory frightened the girls and intimidated the men who worked for him. Beyond this, he was almost always attired in a black leather trench coat designed to suggest some kind of wicked SS affiliation. Herr Framlow thought these accoutrements made him look like an imposing, big-time Nazi and they definitely did produce this effect.

As if all this were not enough, the diminutive metallurgist persistently used erudite Portuguese words that the uneducated people he dealt with did not understand. This served to add an extra layer of intimidation that was not really needed in Framlow's case.

Born in 1916 outside the village of Haderslev, located some forty kilometers north of the German-Danish border, Gerhardt was the son of a Portuguese woman and a Danish dairy man. From his earliest school days, his teachers were amazed by his academic performance, which was not only the highest in his school, but the highest that any of those worthy educators had ever encountered. He was able to teach himself Portuguese, German, and English, as well as elementary differential and integral calculus by the age of fifteen. These subjects were not even offered in his local Gymnasium's three year curriculum.

It should also be mentioned that this undersized lad failed utterly to show promise for the dairy industry, informing his mother and father that he hated cows and their filthy ways. His father and mother accepted this with surprising grace because young Gerhardt had won every academic honor available to secondary school students in the part of Denmark where he lived. His parents were very proud of their little scholar. These honors attracted a scholarship for German-speaking Danes at the prestigious Heidelberg University in Germany where Gerhardt studied mathematics, science and, ultimately, attained a doctorate in the field of physical metallurgy. It might as well also be admitted that this physically challenged Dane had a dairy man's command of the vernacular in both the Danish and Portuguese languages; a vocabulary skill all milkers of cows acquire as soon as they are first swatted in the face by a cow's tail encrusted with a half kilogram of fresh shit.

Young Framlow's enthusiasm for Nazi politics did not arise in his Danish homeland. There is no room for politics on a diary farm. There is room only for the brain-numbing, eternal routine of milking the cows twice a day, seven days a week *ad infinitum*. No, his political views were acquired during his impressionable undergraduate years at Heidelberg University where, in the middle 1930's, there was no shortage of radical campus speakers, virulent National Socialist rabble-rousers, and rallies of all political stripes ranging between the extremes of communism and fascism. It must be admitted that, in spite of his lack of Aryan racial traits, Gerhardt Framlow became excessively Germanized.

On account of his physical limitations, Gerhardt had been rejected by the *Kriegsmarine* in 1939, but soon thereafter in the same year, he was recruited by the German military intelligence organ known as the *Amtsgruppe Ausland* of the *Abwehr*. By this time, he had been transformed into a fanatical Nazi, and with his Doctor of Science degree in metallurgy, he was considered an extremely valuable asset to this particular organization.

For these reasons, coupled with his knowledge of the Portuguese language, he was assigned to Fundão to track production at the Panasqueira mine and coordinate shipments of wolfram concentrates destined for Germany. Doktor Framlow, in fact, controlled all Nazi tungsten activities in Portugal from his small brothel in Fundão and reported directly to the German ambassador, the Baron von Hoyningen-Huene in Lisbon.

The ladies who worked the bar and beds at Doces mostly catered to the needs of men employed at the Panasqueira mine. The majority of these lived in, or nearby, Fundão and they were the primary targets for information related to mine activities. On occasion, these ladies had to deal with Portuguese government officials and members of the secret police who invariably demanded gratis service. Both the proprietor and the ladies accepted this, reluctantly perhaps, as a necessary cost of their operation.

Each girl at Doces received a short, but quite intensive training course at the German embassy located on Campo dos Mártires da Pátria in Lisbon. Here, a German lady of vast expertise, recruited especially for this purpose by the *Abwehr*, taught them the skills of the prostitute and how to elicit information from miners, millworkers, truck drivers, and technical staff of the mine who dealt with tungsten production and shipments. Ladies reporting useful information to Framlow were allowed to keep the one hundred escudo fee for their so-called "quick dates". Those whom did not get information were required to remit half of their well-earned fees to the house, which is to say to the good Doktor Framlow and his Nazi bosses in Lisbon.

Every four or five weeks, the girls rotated to a different brothel run by the *Abwehr* and there were many of these in Portugal, especially in Lisbon and Porto, during the war years. It was a system that worked efficiently, an indispensible requirement for the Third Reich, and, as a result, Herr Doktor Framlow was better informed about technical matters at the Panasqueira mine than the mine superintendent himself.

Naturally, Framlow and MacLorey had extensive dossiers on each other and were perfectly aware of the other man's identity, educational background, and military duties. Nevertheless, the intellectual isolation of Fundão spurred them to engage in the entertaining charade of accepting each other's cover identity. Framlow presented himself as a simple Danish ex-patriot running an honest tavern and MacLorey affected to be a cork-merchant for a consortium of British wine estates.

Because they were equally matched intellectually, both men enjoyed

the repartee, double entendres, and ironies deriving from this charade.

It is even possible that they might have grown to be friends had it not

been for the war. But there was a war in 1940; a deadly, earnest war,

and they were enemies at least in terms of their respective war time

assignments.

Herr Doktor Framlow was rather melancholy on this particular

evening, and not because his books revealed financial losses. Quite the

contrary, Casa dos Doces was making an excellent profit from its

legitimate activities and, of course, even more from its illegitimate

enterprises. No, his grim countenance was due to other causes. The first

occurred some two and a half months back on April 9, 1940 when the

Third Reich invaded his Danish homeland and neighboring Norway. This

was the first event in a string of spectacular Nazi successes in 1940

which included not only the invasions and occupations of Denmark and

Norway, but also the May 27 - June 4 British disaster at Dunkirk and the

unexpected and unpardonable fall of France on June 22.

Of course. no one could have expected tiny, flat Denmark to be

able to resist a well-planned and well-timed German invasion by land, sea, and air, but his mother country was only able to oppose this vicious attack for six hours before capitulation. That was little more than the time needed to milk fifty cows and hose their shit from the floors and walls of the milking parlor. It was just too pathetic for words in any language!

Gerhardt Framlow was not a super patriot for the cause of Danish social democracy, but he was a Dane by birth and culture and he certainly thought his fellow Danes could have put up more resistance than sisteen men killed and twenty wounded. And poor King Christian X, what was to become of him? And speaking of kings, how did his brother Haakon VII, the king of Norway, manage to flee with his royal family, the parliament and fifty tons of Norway's gold bullion to London? The Royal Navy should at least be acknowledged for buying, at a great cost of ships and lives, a few weeks of time before the wicked Germans devoured Norway completely.

Poor King Christian X with only six hours of warning had no alternative but to remain in his palace. But he made it his daily business to ride unaccompanied on his beautiful white horse, Jubilee, through the cheering crowds on the streets of Copenhagen. Framlow, in spite of his Nazi mindset, could not refrain from being proud of these provocative anti-Reich gestures of his king. Of course, the Germans did manage to gobble up Denmark's gold bullion, worth some fifty-nine million US dollars in 1940, so it was very much a case of paying for one's own rape.

As a metallurgist, Framlow appreciated that the motivations behind these invasions of his homeland and Norway was no mere Scandinavian adventures on the part of the Nazis. Germany had to protect their imported iron ore supply mined in arctic Sweden between the small mining towns of Kiruna and Gällivare, and naturally, they had to insure the safe transportation of this ore across Sweden and Norway by rail.

It was a fact there could be no war for Germany without the steel fabricated from neutral Sweden's iron ore. The British understood this as well, but were able to do little more than harass German activities and force Hitler to maintain a very large number of troops in occupied Norway and Denmark to resist a threatened British invasion that never came.

These vital iron ores were carried by special ore hauling ships from the all-weather port of Narvik south down the Norwegian coast, through the protected territorial waters of the so-called "Norwegian Corridor" to the Skagerrak Straight north of Jutland, Denmark. This corridor of safety, guaranteed by Norway's steadfast insistence on a state of neutrality, actually hindered Britain's attempt to save the country from Nazi predation.

Upon reaching the Skagerrak Straight, the German ship captains had to choose whether to travel down the west coast of Denmark directly to Hamburg where the ores could be efficiently carried on inland waterways to the Ruhr and Rhineland. This was the preferred route because it was the most efficient in terms of time and cost, always a paramount consideration for the Germans of this era. But it was also the most dangerous choice in terms of encountering British navel vessels and bombers.

The alternative choice was to sail south along the east coast of Denmark and deliver the ores to the port of Lübeck, Germany. This was considerably safer for the captains because of protection from German airbases established in occupied Denmark. However, this route was considerably less efficient because it required hauling the heavy, bulky ores overland to the industrial centers by the already overburdened German rail system.

However, there was a second and timelier reason for the bordello manager's grim and melancholic mood on this particular evening. This revolved around recent orders from his *Abwehr* chief in Lisbon asking for elimination of Captain MacLorey from the Fundão scene. God only knew how dull and depressing life in Fundão would then become for Herr Doktor Framlow without his nightly encounters with the "cork merchant" from the Isle of Skye. MacLorey was the only person in Fundão, maybe the only one in all of Portugal, who was anywhere close to his own intellectual capacity. Without a doubt, it would be a tragic personal loss for Gerhardt Framlow; almost as bad as the occupation of Denmark after only six hours of resistance.

Framlow overcame his reluctance to perform this unpleasant duty by reminding himself that he was a good Nazi and, of course, everyone knows a good Nazi follows orders, but he had to admit that he did not relish these particular orders.

Rocina Leitão was a new girl, new both to prostitution and to the Casa dos Doces. She was an exceptionally pretty Portuguese rural girl from the small city of Santa Comba Dão and newly graduated from the *Abwehr* finishing school in Lisbon. She had large chestnut-colored eyes, raven hair, perfect teeth, a beautiful complexion and the most enormous breasts you could imagine. These same breasts had created a sensation in certain circles of Santa Comba Dão where it was commonly said that Rocina Leitão had "peaked early". Dreadful entendres of this sort passed for cleverness among the rakes of that good city. Naturally, Rocina was hated by her female classmates who were jealous of her obvious attributes and ostracized the poor girl. The boys, on the other hand, loved her desperately, but they could not refrain from daily sorties they euphemistically called, *"bandos de mãos"*. When these daily and indecorous teenage incursions threatened to become hourly events it became necessary for school officials to step in. After due consideration, it was decided that these particular breasts were sufficiently stimulating, in the eyes of the faculty, to have the poor lass expelled from public school at the tender age of fifteen.

So, in the end, Rocina was forced to leave her village school and her home, but at least her modesty was still intact, if not her brassieres. But she would soon be forced to matriculate into a new and much more serious institution and its curriculum would be far more challenging and indecorous than that of the small school in Santa Comba Dão.

Her parents gave her a pittance of money and a bus ticket, and sent Rocina to a non-existent aunt in Lisbon where her modesty did ultimately suffer as she was compelled to do what was necessary to obtain food and shelter. Perhaps luckily, she was soon picked up by

Abwehr agents and recruited for her present post in Fundão after the requisite training at the German embassy. Naturally, this was all for the greater good of the Third Reich.

It should be mentioned that the name *Rocina* was self-chosen as a professional name by this rural young lady soon after her arrival in Lisbon. It was selected because she thought it sounded sexy and that it meant "sprinkled with dew" in Portuguese, which sounded nice. Of course, she was thinking of the Portuguese verb *rocinar,* which does mean "be-dewed". She had discovered this seldom-used literary word by accident in the very large dictionary housed in her former school library, and she had taken it under her wing for future use.

Not being a scholar, Rocina had failed to consider how closely the phonetics of her new name approached that of *Rocinante* of *Don Quixote* fame which Cervantes had derived from the Spanish noun *rocin*. Needless to say this poor child knew nothing of Cervantes, Spanish nouns, or the dangers lurking in very large dictionaries of any language. But she had at least heard the equivalent Portuguese noun, *rocim*, sometimes used by rural persons to refer to old broken down draft horses, but that was an entirely different word from *Rocina*, at least in her own mind. It might have been an improvement to use a permutation of the name she was baptized with, which was Maria da Fátima da Silva Leitão. But in Portugal, the law forbids prostitutes from using religious names like Maria or Fátima, so, perhaps, *Rocina* was the best choice, after all. It does have a nice sound.

Rocina had been instructed by Senhor Framlow himself earlier in the day to present herself to the big Scotsman after he was drunk and to conduct him to a special bedroom that was normally off limits to the girls and their patrons. Once in that room, she was to take his money, induce him to stand on a small decorative red carpet beside the ornate waiting bed, and pull a bell rope to summon Senhor Framlow. It was suggested that this was part of an elaborate and friendly joke to be played upon the Captain by Doces personnel. This was not something she was taught by the German lady in Lisbon, but that authoritative woman did teach her to obey her whore masters implicitly. So now, on the first day in her new employment, Rocina wanted to appear professional. She wanted to please her new employer and dared not question the motives behind this bizarre request. Senhor Framlow was, after all, a well-educated foreign gentleman.

Captain Colin MacLorey was drinking what he calculated should be his last glass of whisky for the evening. He was drunk, but not so drunk that he was unaware of where he was and his duty to king and country. He thought Framlow was acting a little weird on this particular evening by staring at him over the pages of his account book, but not calling him over for their usual exchange of jocose witticisms. Also the gratis bottle of Talisker scotch from the Isle of Skye was out of character for this crooked little Nazi. But, of course, that in itself was a clever witticism in that it indicated Framlow knew very well he was a native of Skye. MacLorey decided he would have to counter this novel gesture with a bottle of aquavit from Denmark, if one could be obtained in Lisbon.

The drunken Captain MacLorey leisurely approached the table where Framlow was sitting, bringing with him his half-empty bottle of Talisker. He opened a conversation with, *"Boa noite, Senhor Proprietário."*

"Please, stick with the English, Mister Cork Merchant. Your Portuguese does not do you honor," replied the metallurgist with what, at least for Framlow, was a sort of smile. "Sit down and join me in a drink."

"Thank you, Framlow. Would you like to try this bonny excellent Scotch whisky you have so generously presented to me?"

"No, thank you, my friend. Scotch tastes like swamp water to me.

Permit me to offer you the best cognac my humble tavern can provide."

"Yes, of course," returned the Scotsman, taking a chair across from the little Nazi.

"Perhaps you will have some interest in the new girl I have brought in today. She is quite a striking specimen of rural Portuguese beauty and will be making an appearance presently."

"Yes, I am very interested, of course. This has been a bloody difficult day for me," replied the big Brit, hoisting the glass of cognac to his mouth."

"So, I gather that looking at cork trees can be considered a form of physical labor?"

"Yes, certainly, one must assess the quality of the cork, survey the number of trees, then estimate their size and age range, evaluate transportation and labor costs to get the product to market, and finally calculate the net worth of the cork in terms of the projected economic life time of the forest stand. There is a good deal of walking and computation involved, Framlow, and all of it under this beastly Portuguese sun. I assure you, it is nothing like running a bordello from a comfortable chair beneath a ceiling fan and sipping cognac."

"I suppose this is true, but accounting and keeping whores in line and looking well is no child's play, either. Also, they eat more than horses," returned the tavern owner with another small smile appearing between the dangling, mouse-tail mustachios.

"I think that you know by now that I am always offended when you call them whores, Senhor Framlow. I think of them as beautiful wildflowers along the wayside of a Highland path," said MacLorey, playfully feigning indignation.

"Very poetically spoken, indeed, Colin, I did not realize that the current of poetry ran so deeply in the Scottish people."

"An' mon, do ye no ken our illustrious an' bonny poet Bobby Burns?"

"Ah, the famed Scottish brogue, how delightful it is to hear it at last! Yes, I have heard of this Robert Burns, he writes about haggis and such. I find haggis to be a truly revolting dish, but I suppose you were raised on it," Framlow replied, aiming the reflection from his naziesque monocle into the Scotsman's face.

Not one to be intimidated, MacLorey retorted with, "I suppose that you know your surname is an anagram of *wolfram,* which is a strategic wartime commodity mined on a large scale not so far from where we sit."

"Yes, I do know about the wolfram mining. Their heavy trucks send clouds of dust into my establishment almost hourly. However, I have never bothered to consider my surname in terms of anagram permutations. But I must hasten to point out that your own surname is an anagram of *claymore*, the famous two-handed, double-edged Scottish broadsword. I have found that such serendipities as these are rather common in surnames in all languages and, of course, I can take no responsibility for the spelling of a name handed down to me by my forefathers."

The erudite Dane then interrupted his train of thought with, "Oh, now you must take notice, Colin! The new girl has just entered the room. Do you like her?"

At that moment, the new girl, Rocina, approached the table where MacLorey and Framlow were seated. Captain MacLorey was entirely enchanted by both the tight short-sleeved red sweater she was wearing and the fact that Rocina was aiming two of the biggest tits he had ever seen directly at his solar plexus. He stood and managed to mutter, "Good evening, my dear," in English, then realized his mistake and said in Portuguese, "*Boa noite, moça minha.*" Rocina smiled graciously, quite aware that men often lost their train of thought when confronted by her breasts.

"You can speak English if you prefer, Senhor. I can speak some, but not so well. Will the Senhor buy me a drink?" she volunteered in English, flavored with a strong Portuguese accent.

"Yes, certainly. You are new here, I believe. What is your name?" he asked with his eyes still riveted on her chest as they moved from the table towards the bar.

Herr Doktor Framlow appeared to return to his accounting, but in truth he paid minute attention to the progressing romantic drama developing between Rocina and Captain MacLorey.

"My name is Rocina and yes, this is my first night in Casa dos Doces, Senhor," she replied with a friendly smile that revealed her beautiful white teeth while ignoring his lustful staring.

"Rocina, that is a very beautiful name indeed." Evidently, MacLorey was as ignorant as the girl when it came to Cervantes and Spanish nouns. MacLorey ordered two glasses of cognac from the bartender and immediately resumed his salacious campaign.

The Scotsman, who was entirely ignorant of Portuguese history, opened his assault with, "I recall studying 'The Age of the Navigators' in school and the account of the heroic voyage of Vasco da Gama, the famous Portuguese navigator. He was the first European to reach India by sea, I believe."

"Yes, I think you are correct, Ssenhor," returned Rocina, who was no better informed on this subject than the big foreigner. A brief and desultory historical discussion followed that is not worth repeating here as virtually all of it was in error. But this exchange did serve the purposes of both parties to "break the ice", as people often say.

After what seemed to be an appropriate period of inane conversation, which is to say two or three minutes, Captain MacLorey got down to the business at hand by saying, "Would five hundred escudos allow me into your bed, Rocina?" This was uttered with a hopeful boyish grin that experience had taught the Captain was very effective at charming ladies.

"But of course, but you know that it is too much, no?"

"It is not too much to get my hands on those lovely tits, Rocina."

"I think you will want four hands for my tits, Senhor," she answered with a coquettish wink and, turning, led the way toward the special bedroom. MacLorey followed her closely, of course, barely able to resist the urge to skip like an overjoyed child.

Once inside the specially assigned room, she took his money and laid it in sight on the lamp table. Captain MacLorey's hands were instantly occupied with her breasts as she gently coaxed him toward the red carpet. He was nearly in position when he began disrobing at a furious rate, and in no time at all he was in the bed naked and urgently beckoning Rocina to join him.

Rocina, for her part, did not give up on her assignment, but it was clear that she would have to deal with the Scotsman's needs before anything else. She removed her clothes methodically and as sensually as she could, while making quite sure the gentleman on the bed was observing every move she made. Rocina removed her bra last of all with her back turned to her guest and then, turning quickly toward the anxious Brit, she leaped for the bed with a playful giggle. Of course, she made quite certain that she cleared the mysterious ornamental red carpet which was now occupied by MacLorey's crumpled trousers and a pair of large wingtips.

The act itself was not particularly noteworthy in Rocina's rather limited experience. She had actually expected a more satisfying performance from a man with MacLorey's physical attributes and reputation at Casa dos Doces. But this disappointment was blunted to some degree by her recollection of a timeless Portuguese proverb worthy of Cervantes that said, "When it comes to sex, the whole hillside is not covered in spice." Apparently, Rocina would have to content herself with this wisdom of the ages, but at least the world would continue to spin.

After the act was physically over, Rocina redirected her concentration to her peculiar assignment. After all, the joke must be played out to the end and she must not disappoint her new master. She rose from the ornate bed after the requisite post-coital respite and quickly began donning her clothes. Naturally, she kept herself away from the red carpet and observed the Captain's moves very closely. He sat on the edge of the bed with his feet on this same carpet putting his legs through his trousers. Then, when he stood up to fasten them, Rocina quickly sprang for the bell rope and pulled it as instructed by the worthy Senhor Framlow.

There was a distinct and eerie mechanical click and the look on the Scotsman's face transformed instantly from smiling fatigued gratification to shocked surprise as he and his large wingtip shoes disappeared through the floor.

The last thing Captain MacLorey saw was Rocina's back-lighted and rapidly-receding face framed in a black square; he saw this pretty face and, of course, those enormous breasts..

Rocina Leitão

Dr. Lowell was born and raised on a small dairy farm outside of Modesto, California. He attended high school in Glendora, California and subsequently received a B.S. degree in geology from San Jose State. His passion for rocks and minerals led him to the New Mexico Institute of Mining and Technology in Socorro where he received a Ph.D degree in geology three years later. A long academic career followed at Southeast Missouri State and the University of Texas-Arlington that included numerous consulting jobs for mineral industry. Dr. Lowell has published more than 100 scientific works but the present story marks his third foray into the world of fiction. He reads widely and is especially fond of 19th century classic literature. His favorite books are *Les Miserables* and *My Ántonia*. Dr. Lowell and his wife Vicki live in Arlington, Texas; their two adult children live nearby.

www.ingramcontent.com/pod-product-compliance
Lightning Source LLC
Chambersburg PA
CBHW020322150626
46552CB00022B/3153